THE CHRONICLES
OF
LOVE & PAIN

MARIO GIVENS

The Chronicles of Love & Pain

Copyright 2018 By Mario Givens

ISBN: 978-0-692-19879-7

Printed in the United States of America

PREFACE

This Poetry book is for everyone. I don't have a specific audience because we all experience love and pain somewhere down the line of our lives. In other words, I am writing this book for people who can relate to being in love and how the feeling makes them feel so secure and happy. I am also writing it for the people who experience pain and hurt from fail relationships due to hardships of love. My mission is to empower those who wants to take another shot at love and also those who are still in love to continue to build a prosperous union.

DEDICATION

Dear World,

I want to dedicate this book to all the people who supported me and continue to support me on making my dreams come true. I'm a traditional type of person and I never want to leave out anyone because it was so many people who motivated me and inspired me to write this poetry book. With that being said, I just want to sincerely and humbly leave you with my heart and soul.

Introduction

I never thought love can feel so good and also hurt so bad when you are dealing with someone that you consider special to your heart. Have you ever been hurt? Have you ever been so in love you couldn't live without that person? This poetry book was written to not only showcase poetry but to grasp the readers so they can visualize the challenges of being in love and the pain of love. The Chronicles of Love &Pain will display many moments of the author Mario Givens experiences.

TABLE OF CONTENTS

BON VOYAGE

I can't wait to lay on the beach chairs

Relax my mind

Enjoy the days and nights of fun

The cold drinks

A kiss from the sun

I'm so calm

The ocean is blue

It's telling a story

While the dolphins swim by

The sea birds fly overhead

It's time to go to the jacuzzi

The warm water soothes me

I'm so calm

The band plays some jazz

We decide to take a walk

A short stroll on the deck

Then we stop

Admiring the view as the wind blew

You gave me a slow kiss on my neck

I'm so calm

Determine to be in the moment

Grateful to relax with you

A night on the love boat

Hopefully I'll fall in love with you.

DETOUR

I want to leave

Go somewhere Chaos don't live

Where love is the only option

A place where you get what you give

Life is a beautiful thing

It can bring so much happiness

Many joyful moments

Like a kid on a swing

That's where I want to go

A place where you can be free

Nights without negativity

The Stars line up with the moon

I need to get there soon

Where's words are calm when they speak

I need to take this ride

First I got to get off this confused street.

CARNATIONS

Can I give you this?

Place it in a vase

Your eyes are so beautiful

A soft kiss

They will give you good luck

Pure love is my feelings

You deserve this gift

I admire your heart

I adore your smile

Each color has a meaning

Like you are defined by many

I'm deeply in love with you

I present you with these carnations

Enjoy this gift from God.

DIAMONDS

Do you take this ring?

Cherish it with love

Hold it close to your heart

It has values

It represents my love

A dedication from my spirit

It symbolizes my feelings

The carats are my truth

When it shines that's my loyalty

You are my gem

A stone that shows my longevity

My future is now

For better and worse

A queen has her jewelry.

SIMPLICITY

I love this

The touch of your hand

It makes me happy

Your eyes are glowing

I got butterflies

It's a crush feeling

Love is so simple

When your kiss makes me smile.

SOUL-MATE

We are as one

I can feel your pain

Your heart beats my same rhythm

When you smile

My teeth show the same way

You finish my sentences

My true love

You are my companion

My alter ego

A kindred spirit

I accept ones promise

You are everything my heart desires

My help mate

My souls in a peaceful state

Everything my heart desires

Inspired by your motivation

Our love making houses passion

I trust you with my life.

ECSTASY

I want to take this trip to paradise

A feeling of euphoria

A sense of joyfulness

I'm in a trance

Intoxicated from your romance

It's like I'm in a frenzy

Cloud nine is like seventh heaven

You give me so much happiness

I'm blessed

Delighted by the opportunity

The passion over takes me

A feeling of enchantment

I'm caught up in a rapture

I'm content to be full of joy

This passion came to fruition.

CANDLE

Your smile is radiant

The fire inside your soul

It creates an aura of peace

You are a torch when I'm around

I want to place you in my heart

So, when I melt

A scent of love owns the room

You really purify my spirit

I'm hurt when the flame goes out

I'll light another one

Our love stays lit forever.

TRANQUILITY OF MY LIFE

It's quiet
A sacred moment
I ponder
I kind of wonder
Is this real
The feeling of stillness
Serenity calms restfulness
When I'm around you
My composure has stability
I'm grateful to have you
It's a glimpse of harmony
You are part of me
I have a peace of mind
My life has some order
It's lawful to love you.

SINCERITY

When I look into your eyes

I'm humble God place you here

Grateful to adopt you in my life

I'll cherish every moment

I'm ecstatic by your presence

I'm hypnotized by your beauty

You are telling me a story of love

I read your spirit

It's a genuine feeling

I'm so secure from your trust

It's warmth inside my soul

I dedicate my love to your heart

I received my clarity

A wholehearted feeling, I have

You complete me.

EVERLASTING PAIN

Why can't this hurt leave?

I'm in a place where I'm afraid

My love was disrespected

It wasn't protected

I'm vulnerable

Distant from security

I lost my trust for you

I'm suffering from a spasm of deceit

Agony puts pressure on my chest

Grieving from the death of this relationship

There's a laceration to my heart

I'm wounded

Abused from physical sorrow

My misery becomes torn

When will this hardship end?

I need a cure before fatigue sets in.

ROAD TRIP

Let's pack this bag

Make a stop to get gas

We got to take a journey

Go to a place of peace

Destination with you is what I needed

The road is clear

Our communication has clarity

We are in a space of compatibility

I switch lanes

You held my hand

Look across the console

I look your way

Then our favorite song plays on the radio

I begin to smile

Then you start to sing

The happiness has taken over us

We exit to weeks of recreation

The car stops at rest and recuperation.

MOVIE DATE

I'm a little nervous

She's worth this night

Did I over dress?

What would she look like?

I knock on the door

She opens

Beauty was in front of me

I gave her hug

We proceeded to the car

I open her door

Then we arrive at the theater

I surprise her with a comedy movie

Laughter is key

Do you want some popcorn?

I prefer mints and a drink

The previews is my favorite part

We took our seats

It's showtime

We give each other looks

A slow soft peck breaks the tension

The credits will establish our status.

SUPPORT

Even during a stressful day
You are here
Even when I'm down
You are here
Even when I'm scared
You are here

My thoughts are quiet
I believe you are here
My voice shakes
I believe you are here
My tears stop falling
I believe you are here

During my hardships
You stayed here
During my happiest moments
You stayed here

During confusing times
You stayed here.

MY LEGACY

I believe in us

The possibility of forever

I cherish your footsteps

Stability has a home with you

I'm in love with longevity

I'm committed to security

I'm secluded from lost

I'm dedicated to your heart

You are the reason for my happiness

Life is real when you are near

I want to kneel to you

Propose my soul to you

Engage my love to you

Eternity waits when you say I do.

DEATH OF TRUTH

A night where the air was cold
Trust died this night
It told a story
Deceit was the ultimate glory
Then the wind blew
The air is getting colder
Many stars lost their shine
The moon pretended to love
Then a cloud blocks her view
Escaping from the pain
The death of truth.

FOREHEAD KISS

My affection for you

It shows through this kiss

Placing my thoughtful lips

Embracing your love

My energy creates an aura

Your brain receives my heart

You are safe in my character

Forever is an art

Can you feel my thoughts?

My respect is the goal

I'm in love with your soul

We have passion

Making love when our eyes close.

FAITHFUL LOVE

I believe in you
The moments where I trust you
Passion resurrected inside me
My love is strong

I pledge allegiance to your heart
My loyalty has no suspicion
I'm confident in our commitment
There's no resentment
I have the assurance when it comes to you

You accept all my flaws
There's hope for longevity
My fidelity respects yours
I have courage to fall in love with you

There's certainly
I'm positive my heart is happy

Through rain or shine

I will take the oath to love you

My soul will prosper

Our lives will have an unvarnished truth.

I'M SORRY

Your eyes are saddened
Did I hurt you?
Made you feel less than happiness
I'm sorry

When I look at you
The angry possess your being
I didn't think you will cry
I'm sorry

What can I do to make you smile?
Don't be confused by my actions
Your calm validates me
I'm sorry

Please forgive me
The happiness can return
Your soul reminds me of care
Thanks for accepting my apology.

MUSICAL CONCERT

Have you ever wanted something so bad?

That it made you cry

Made your heart wither

Then you saw her

She gave you life

She replenishes your soul

Her eyes were the missing shine

She glows

Her voice is the piano

My spirit is the audience

Our time is the instruments

When you hug me

I feel like I'm in a duet

A concert

The fans are the angels

Cupid is the applauds

Our stage is holy matrimony.

GOD BLESS ME

I stop asking

I decided to let God bless me

He molds a creation from clay

Not only took a rib

He also took part of my heart

He communicated to her through his breath

Her eyes open

The first person she saw was me

I guess love at first sight is true

It was like a scene in a movie

Cupid shot his bow

First one miss

So, I kneeled to the floor

Then he struck again

Peace was still

She smiles

I smile

The arrow hit her soul

It went through my spirit

Then years later

The music plays

Many people clap

Happiness was the destination

She carries my name

Months later

She carries our claim

A family was born

When I prayed to God what I wanted.

A FLIGHT FOR LOVE

I kept looking up at the sky

Wondering will you land

Hoping you realize

I'm waiting at the gate

I'm patiently nervous

I got turbulence in my heart

You got turbulence from the clouds

Then I felt you at baggage claim

You walk towards my car

Then it hit me

An angel in my presence

I felt calm

You felt warm

The breeze balance us

It felt like a completed puzzle

A king embraces his queen

You whisper in my ear

I receive your words

My scent kisses your nasal

Your hands grasp my back

Passion was born

A possibility was form

Our goals need execution

I want a future

You want freedom

We both have a destination

Hopefully we can travel together

Let's plan a trip to forever.

Non-fictional Moment

She's So beautiful

It's like a blessing from God

That smile

It's like a vision from the creator

You brighten up a sad part of me

That lonely side

Then I wonder who is this woman

Her words penetrated my soul

From every verb

To every noun

I'm curious to want to know her

Create a sentence

Write a paragraph from her beauty

I got lost in her eyes

I'm mesmerize

She seems so mysterious

That my thoughts wonder what's she thinks about

I can't lie

I want to be a thought
Then I think about how smooth she is
The times I got the honor to be near her
The energy was calm
It's when your soul and spirit have balance
Then I picture her lips on mines
My hand rubs through her hair
Her hands rub my face
We both understand this sacred place
Some dreams come true
Others remain a clue
Then her words spark my mind
Inspired by someone who shares the same gift
Motivated by the talent
I continue to wait for her
So, I can read more
Take a vacation inside her personal book
Each poem is a chapter
I don't want them to end
What motivates her?
I'm Curious on her glossary
I wanted to be a blurb to her book
So can I be in your index
I don't expect things

I'm cautious with my heart
Definitely need to fix my self-issues
That way I have no flaws
Opportunities don't often come
If my mental thought gets a knock
I want to make sure she understands
She will be the only one.

AN ANGEL SOARS

When I look up at the sky

I saw you fly towards me

It was like an eagle soar

I'm really anxious

Definitely a little nervous

Your wings flap your love

As you glide

The birds smile

Then you landed

You embrace me with a hug

Then I kiss your lips

A tear falls down my cheek

That's when I knew my heart was in love

An angel held my hand

You recited your feelings to me

I responded my peace

Then you said I have to leave

More tears fell

You begin to wipe my face
The words you stated of us being forever
It really melted my soul
Then you flew away
A feather laid on the ground
I will cherish this heavenly day.

GRACEFUL

It was a cool winter night

You cross my mind

I was wondering did I cross yours

I wanted to see you

Your beauty attracts me

A frame should hold your face

Your skin is so delicate

A silky-smooth look

It gives a pleasant glow

You are the definition of grace

Your eyes can persuade me

temptation has distracted my focus

Then I visualize your hair

It shows your modesty

It's like a sense of honor

Then when you speak

Every verb and noun peacefully sound

Leaving every word full of affection

I desire your presence

Your companionship is needed
I'm eager to see you
When you arrive
Your give me stability
I have self- assurance.

DESTINED TO LOVE

I fell in love with you

It was a destination

Only my heart wanted to go

A place of peace

Determine to be happy

Your smile brings me calm

I wither in your arms

I'm comfortable

Relax from the opportunity to love

Intoxicated by your soul

I'm attracted to your ability to love me

Our reflections describe happiness

I'm confident our growth is the next destination.

PROTECTED

I get lonely when you not here
Your aura represents peace
Your soul is dedicated to me
My spirit becomes inspired
An internal happiness
I'm secured by your presence.

A BEAUTIFUL VASE

Just a moment to think

An opportunity to speak

So, I pause

Measuring the knowledge, I share

Patient with care

Realizing a rose needs water

Your smile is the sun

Your eyes are the nourishment

So, I pause again

Thinking about putting you in a vase

My heart is the table

You will rest on my chest.

A RELATIONSHIP WITH THE MOON

Another glance at the moon

My eyes are in love

I'm in a trance

A particular stance

I want a chance

To express my heart

To impress your guard

So, you can lower it

Secure from the possibility of my soul

I'm protecting you

Can I have this moment?

To display my feelings

Then you smile

Your rays touch me

Creating a warm aura

My body feels numb

You are so beautiful

I'm poise from your grace

The light shines in my space
You are the telescope to my world.

RETURN MY LOVE

A slow kiss

That captures my lips

It's amazing how you can love

Then she's gone

Left me with a wish

I truly miss

The days where the nights were great

Her passion contains me

It symbolizes classical moments

A romantic embrace

Our hands connect

Then our eyes fall in love

She smiles

I smile

We dance to our heartbeats

The perfect tune

Happiness over takes the sky

Then I realize she's gone

Will she come back

I miss her

I pray she become the reality of my wish.

SHE PLAYS A SONG WITH HER BEAUTY

Have you ever touched your chest?

Felt an irregular beat

My heart is anxious

Nervous from the glance

She's beautiful

Like a slow melody

The rhythm has a peaceful tune

Her beauty completes my eyes

She's like a jazz album

With a touch of blues

I love her

A woman who has a soul of a piano

Each key represents her character

When I'm around her

My spirit feels like a symphony

I'm grateful for her beauty.

A FRUITFUL DAY

It's a summer day

I plan a perfect date

The sun is Shining

You can hear the birds chirp

I have the blanket

A basket with fruit

As she appears

The clouds disappear

The sky is clear

It's blue like the ocean

Then she sits

We talk

Laughter takes over the time

Then I wash the fruit

I slice apples

Then peel a banana

I gave her a peck

Then welcome her soft lips with a strawberry

She tells me thank you

You are welcome, I replied

Then I fed her grapes

She feeds me grapes

We laugh some more

Life can't get no better

We are healthy and happy

She loves me

I love her

We lay back

Enjoying our day

The wind blows a cool breeze

We are in love

She placed her head on my chest

This day was amazing

To know you have all the gifts from God.

LOVE

I love you

I'm so in love with you

I want the world to know I love her

I'm so in love with her

I really love her

Does she love me?

Does she really love me?

Does she want the world to know she love me?

WE ARE MEANT

What matters to me is I have you

We are meant

The seas have waves because it's meant

The stars shine because it's meant

The rain makes puddles because it's meant

We make love because it's meant

Destiny is clear

We are together forever because it's meant.

UNCERTAINTY

Please don't go

Leave your bags on the floor

I apologize

I accept the blame

The issues are me

I put you through this shame

Can you forgive me?

My hurt penetrates your cure

I made you unsure

I had you questioning my loyalty

I respect our bond

Give me another chance

I dedicate my soul to your security.

THE CAUSE TO MY FOREVER

God created an earthly angel when he molded you

When he blew breath in your lungs, I prayed he thought

about you being in my life.

You can capture my inner peace when I think of you.

I'm blessed to be a pillar to your soul

You are the crown that sits on my heart.

A THOUGHTFUL GETAWAY

You are like a vision of grace

I saw you in a dream

I didn't count sheep's

They were hearts

Everyone symbolizes our bond

You so full of color

Similar to the mountains in Peru

Let's climb together

Make love on the hills

As the sun kisses the cliffs

An eagle emerges from a tree

The skies are clear

Only the wind hugs our souls

I love you

This dream I adore

I don't want to wake

Anxious to want more.

Inner Love

It's strange how I can love you

Many ways I can love you

Not like the roses are red

But the violets can be blue

It just seem so strange

How much I love you

Then I realize

You are like poetry

The words I recite

The rhythm of my flow

The comfort at night

Why love so complicated

It has many levels

Then i buried my feelings inside my hurtful grave

I'm resurrected

Return to love with hope

With the determination to learn more

I want to be the best man

Sitting on a throne of security
I am in Love with my thoughts.

LOCKSMITH

I wish I could wipe your tears away

Place them in a safe

So, you don't have to use them no more

Your pain needs a cure

It's my love

My security to your life

Only God have the passcode to your lock

You are safe in my arms

I'll protect your heart

WHY ARE YOU SAD?

Your happiness lays inside your soul

It's trap behind the glory

That protects your character

Dig deep

Find the glow that lost it shine

Your inner rays need motivation

That way it can spark inspiration

Then your happiness will burst out your spirit.

SECURING A MOMENT

It was a long relaxing night

This walk on the beach secure my feelings

We both discuss our future

My heart attracted your heart

I'm determined to hold your hands

Then look into your eyes

I want to hold you in my arms

Then accept the moon lights

Can I express my feelings?

I fell in love with you

Your smile hypnotized me

Put me in a love trance

This is where I want to be.

THE WAIT FOR LOVE

I love you from my spirit

There are days where I don't want to

wait till next lifetime to be with you,

but if that's all I have to hold on to then

I'll be waiting on Venus

by the craters for you.

A WARM LOVELY NIGHT

I want to make love to you

Right after we sip some hot chocolate

Laying in front of the chimney

I gaze into your eyes

You gaze into my eyes

The warmth from the fireplace creates security

I kiss your hand

Then I tell you I love you

I understand your wanting of satisfaction

So I proceed to caress your soul

The rhythm of your heart

Defends my heart beat

I'm connected to your spirit

We make love till the fire stop burning.

LONGEVITY OF PAIN

All I ever wanted was to love you

It seemed like I failed you

I wasn't the leader

I was the follower

We both was doom from the start

I didn't play my part

Indecisive on my role

I refuse to get better

Insecure about my soul

I wasn't dedicated

I anticipated

Things would be better

I remain stagnant

Mentally secluded from the truth

I didn't know how to love

I gave you years

You gave me years

We forgot about just loving
Now all we have is forever tears.

BRANCHES

You can now replace your broken wings

Soar to a place of tranquility

Then land on a branch of peace

Just remember since you are free

Don't break nobody else's wings

We all are searching for that branch to land on.

MEDICINE

When I found pain
I embrace it
Tried to understand it
Then I research it
To find out she needs Love

CRYING PAIN

I fell in love with a dream

To the point where I woke up

Serenade by ballads of screams

I'm hurt

Shattered by the thoughts of love

I need to be distant

Healing is my only agenda

These cries create waterfalls

My face looks like a lake

Each tear is like a boat

It sails down my cheek

Saddens strikes my heart

I'm stuck in a zone

What can I do?

Why is this happening?

I'm a living tear

My shadow are puddles from pain

I need comfort

Can someone come and wipe my hurt away?

HURTFUL DAMSEL

When I saw her

She was like a damsel in distress

Her face was saddened by trouble

A look of worry

I wanted to rescue her emotions

Then secure her heart with love

Her tears suggest her need for help

I decided to confront her pain

Excuse me, are you ok?

Is there something I can do?

She replies heartbreak consumes her life

When she looks up cupid flew

Left her alone an afraid

Then I reach for some tissue

I pray you will be well

It will take time

Thank you for your concern

Before I proceeded to walk away

I told her it will get better

Please believe and pray

She smile and said thanks again
Hopefully I'll be ok one day.

SEARCHING

I've lost things all my life

I've found things all my life

I Just wish sometimes I can stop losing and find forever love

The type of love that makes magical moments

Where hurt disappears with a stroke of a peaceful wand

A snap of a soulful finger then love appears with sincerity

I want togetherness

I need support to create support

A relationship full of highlights

Where destiny can make love to possibility

Times where happiness remains happy

I want to be secluded from sadness

Only she can inspire my heart to beat

Her motivation forces my lungs to breathe

I love her

I really need her

I'm tired of being lost

I beg cupid to shoot me

Let the arrow strikes my vision

I'm ready to stop searching

Will she appear?

My offering is waiting for her acceptance.

DREAMS

It reminded me of a dream

I was lost inside of love

I was capture by cupid's arrow

My heart was soft like a cloud

It was like my spirit was free like a bird

I begin to walk through the forest

Then I stop to admire trust

The trees were full of life

Each branch was a moment of honesty

Many leaves gave me a since of determination

I knew that love had a place me here

Never in a million years I would be this

I stop again I kneel for berries

I can hear many sounds

When I look up

She was standing in front of me

A smile that produce sunshine through the trees

Her scent was like flowers on the forest floor

I stood in front of her

This was a greet of forever

Happiness grew with every stroll

Our voices remain peacefully with humble words

I love her

Does she love me?

Hopefully I will get my answer when I fall asleep again.

BROKEN-HEARTED

I felt the arrow when it struck me

The pain brought tears to my eyes

I cried many nights

Puddles consume my pillows in the morning

My soul is mourning

The lies are burning

Truth ran out when the deceit overcame me

I can feel the bitterness

Agony devours my character

Remorse never came to ease the pain

It feels like a sense of hopelessness

My emotions weren't valued

I had the impression love wouldn't hurt

That it would be the peace to storms that

produce clouds of hurt

I felt the letdown

The inability to fight depression

My spirit feels like grief kisses distress

I lack understanding
These feelings I have displays sorrow
I snatch the arrow out my heart
Medicine is needed to function tomorrow.

ULTIMATE LOVE

I know that I love you unconditional, because I forgave you without you apologizing.

HURTFUL KISS

When we kiss

I didn't feel the energy

My eyes were close

When I open them, yours were open

I guess you were kissing someone else in your mind.

RESTFUL SLEEP

As she lay

Her dreams seem peaceful

She presents a smile

It's like she can feel my presence

Her aura consists of security

The moon kisses her forehead

Her calmness displayed a smell of lavender

Every breath she takes is like an angel whispering in her ear

Her hands are like a rose in heavens garden

She's so beautiful

This night she deserves this opportunity to rest

I'm honored to have her lay next to me

It's very enchanting to fall in love with her silence.

SOMEONE ELSE'S ARMS

He captures your soul

Your eyes left me and join him

Your heart transferred beats

Many smiles brighten his day

He's given you many memories of joy

I took a few moments to dwell on you leaving

Then I glance at your happiness

My time has come to move on

His clock of love begins at 12:00am

I didn't appreciate your love

I took your heart for granted

When I suppose to made love to you

I made love for the moment

My chances are no longer

I pray your happiness continues with peace.

Quiet Rain

As I sit in my puddle of sorrow

All I can vision is my love leaving my life

The thoughts of one extra night

Holding you close

A slow peck to show I love you

Many memories create a drizzle on my face

My heart is shattered

I'm miserable in this sunken place

I wish I could tell you my feelings

Each tear has its own story

The puddle that's form is a pool of hurt

I never felt this way

No words can express my soul

I really need to pray

Can God give me an umbrella of comfort

Take this storm away.

THE PERFECT RIB

It was you that perfected me

The night God place you in my life

I was reborn

Your inspiration was like a piece of fresh fruit

You completed my journey

The ultimate goal wasn't accomplished

until you motivated me

I'm proud to love you endlessly

When I see you my heart melts

Your presence makes me feel like

I'm lying in the garden of Eden

I feel completed

When I'm sleep my soul is at peace

Knowing you are part of me

We are side to side

Equal as one in the eyes of God.

TOMORROW

It was a warm breezy night

I went to sleep

My dreams were sacred

So many thoughts that played a movie

I couldn't wait for the morning

The moment to share with you

A glimpse in your eyes

Your smile warms me like a cup of coffee

The sound of your voice eases my soul

My spirit is anxious to admire your beauty

Then you calm me when your hug me

We can start our day with love

So, our night can rest

Knowing Another tomorrow will come to be with you.

ADMIRATION

A night of passion

Feelings was told with penetration

My heart was satisfied

Her heart was satisfied

We became friends with kisses

I admire her pecks

As they touch my body

My soul relaxes for the night

She stares in my eyes

My eyes whispers tears as she says she loves me

The moment has pass

I will fall asleep

Knowing cupid arrow

Made her fall in love with me.

INTERNAL PAIN

Have you ever felt pain?

The hurt describes your aura

The days seems longer

Many nights weaken me from the pain

My heart skips beats

The sadness in my soul is overwhelming

I'm concern about my happiness

Too many distant moments

I can feel myself being sheltered

It begins to rain

My eyes are sensitive to the sun

This spirit of mines is drowning

What's going to happen to me?

I don't want to be hurt anymore

Can someone help me?

Do anyone understand the hurt I bear?

I'm running out of patience

I just want to be happy again.

IT WAS YOU

Once upon a time

I felt comfort

My pain was at ease

I never would've question you

Then the story change

The words wasn't the same

I begin to stress over you

Many nights tears capture my face

Feeling very empty in my space

You disappointed me

Then you disrespected my heart

Neglected the truth I brought to your lies

I'm stuck in a place of uncertainty

Visualizing why this is happening

Then the sun shine on me

Made me realize you were the clouds that block my light.

JUDGEMENT DAY FOR LOVE

You lied to me

The words that were use aren't valid

Truth was a game

The love wasn't real

I can't believe my hurt

I'm shattered

You disrespected my heart

I feel ashamed

I'm shattered more

This feeling is overwhelming

I didn't deserve this

My happiness left when my smile cried

Why did you lie to me?

My soul died

It left my body

Descended into another space

I'm lost for words

There's no coming back from this

Love judgment is the only place.

No more confusion

This can't be life

You put your all into another

Then your feelings are neglected

It's a time to reflect

I can't keep being disrespected

Why is this happening?

I'm wondering

A time of confusion

Trust no longer lives here

My thoughts create thoughts

I'm trying to find answers

The questions outweigh my mind

Why is this happening?

I ponder drastically

I found the answer

It's time to move on.

I LET GO

I'm leaving

Going to a place where love don't hurt

Where feelings don't matter

I'm tired

I have no more beats in my heart

My tears reverse back into my eyes

I'm very certain about my choice

I can't stay where I'm not wanted

I'm saying goodbye

It's time to leave uncertainty

My destiny is waiting for my arrival

She's standing with her arms wide open

It's time to accept my truth

God wants me to be happy

I can't go against his orders

It's time to regain my happiness again.

SPEECHLESS THOUGHTS

Another night where I whisper to myself

She chose someone else

Why worry anymore

Who comes to ease your pain?

This the time to reinvent yourself

You can't hold on to someone who move on

I have no more tears

This the moment to recycle the hurt

Your smile means more than your sadness

Your truth will arrive

You can't think about the lies

Amending of your heart starts now.

THE END

CONNECT WITH MARIO GIVENS

ACROSS SOCIAL MEDIA PLATFORMS

FACEBOOK

INSTAGRAM

TWITTER

TO CHECK OUT ALL MY BOOKS + FOR

BOOKING INFO VISIT

MY WEBSITE OR EMAIL

MARIOGIVENS@YAHOO.COM

WWW.MARIOGIVENS.INFO

AS WELL AS

And anywhere books are sold.